PUFFIN BOOKS

Hop It, Duggy Dog!

D1147344

Hop It, Duggy Dog!

Brian Ball

Illustrated by
Lesley Smith

PUFFIN BOOKS

For Rachel

PUFFIN BOOKS

Published by the Penguin Group

Penguin Books Ltd, 80 Strand, London WC2R 0RL, England

Penguin Putnam Inc., 375 Hudson Street, New York, New York 10014, USA

Penguin Books Australia Ltd, Ringwood, Victoria, Australia

Penguin Books Canada Ltd, 10 Alcorn Avenue, Toronto, Ontario, Canada M4V 3B2

Penguin Books India (P) Ltd, 11 Community Centre, Panchsheel Park, New Delhi – 110 017, India

Penguin Books (NZ) Ltd, Cnr Rosedale and Airborne Roads, Albany, Auckland, New Zealand

Penguin Books (South Africa) (Pty) Ltd, 24 Sturdee Avenue, Rosebank 2196, South Africa

Penguin Books Ltd, Registered Offices: 80 Strand, London WC2R 0RL, England

www.penguin.com

First published by Hamish Hamilton Ltd 1989
Published in Puffin Books 1996
5 7 9 10 8 6

Text copyright © Brian Ball, 1989
Illustrations copyright © Lesley Smith, 1989
All rights reserved

Printed and bound in China by Leo Paper Products Ltd

British Library Cataloguing in Publication Data
A CIP catalogue record for this book is available from the British Library

ISBN 0–140–38158–9

Duggy Dog stretched out on the rug. He was tired. All night long the thunder had crashed and boomed. The wind had howled, and the rain had gone *squish-slash* on the window-panes.

How could a dog sleep through all that noise?

"I'm tired," he yawned. "It's time for a snooze."

Then Mrs Smith came in with the vacuum-cleaner.

Wuzz-wuzz-barumm! it went. *Wumm-wuzz-waaaa!*

"Hop it, Duggy Dog," said Mrs Smith. "It's morning, and I've got my cleaning to do."

"Uh-oh," said Duggy Dog. "I know. Out!"

Out into the garden he went. But the sun was shining now, and there was a warm patch by the shed.

Duggy Dog closed his eyes, and his tail went *thump-thump* on the ground.

"Sleep," he yawned. "Good."

The tabby kitten from next door was in
the bushes. She saw Duggy Dog's tail
going *thump-thump*. Out came her sharp
claws as she jumped on Duggy Dog's tail.

8

"*Wuff!*" said Duggy Dog. "Who's that?"

He opened his eyes, and saw the tabby kitten.

"I like you, Duggy Dog," she said. "You never get cross with me, do you?"

"Never," growled Duggy Dog.

The tabby kitten purred at him. Off she went to find someone else to jump at.

Duggy Dog closed his eyes, and in a
moment or two he was snoozing
peacefully. But not for long.

"Wake up, Duggy Dog!" cheeped a
chirpy little voice. "Please!"

Duggy Dog opened his eyes. He saw a
baby blackbird cheeping at him. She
looked very sorry for herself.

"How do I fly, Duggy Dog?" she said.
"I keep trying, but I can't remember
how."

Duggy Dog didn't know either. He had never tried to fly. He was thinking about it when the mother blackbird came down with a loud *squawwwkkk!*

"Flap!" she told her baby. "Flap like this!"

The baby blackbird flapped her wings. It was easy!

"I can fly now, Duggy Dog," she said. "Goodbye!"

Duggy Dog called goodbye to the
baby blackbird and said he was glad she
could fly. Off she flew with the mother
blackbird.

Then Duggy Dog yawned twice and closed his eyes again.

He was nearly asleep when a croaky little voice said, "Are you asleep, Duggy Dog?"

It didn't sound like the tabby kitten
from next door. Was it the baby blackbird
again? Duggy Dog didn't want to open
his eyes just yet.

"Is that you, little blackbird?" he yawned.

"No," said the croaky little voice. "It's me. I was a tadpole last week, but look at me now."

Duggy Dog opened his eyes. It was a new frog. It had a new, shiny skin and long, green legs. The new frog hopped up off the ground.

"Watch me, Duggy Dog," he said.

"I'd rather go back to sleep," Duggy Dog told him.

The new frog laughed. "You can sleep
any old time, Duggy Dog. Watch this!"
And he jumped right over Duggy Dog.
Then he jumped back again. And again.
Duggy Dog sighed. Couldn't a dog get
any sleep in his own garden?

First, it was the kitten and her sharp
little claws. Then it was the baby
blackbird who had forgotten how to fly.
And now it was a hoppity new frog with
legs three sizes too big.

Hop! it went over him again. And *hop!*
back again.

"Wouldn't you like to hop off to see all the other new frogs?" said Duggy Dog.

But the new frog didn't know where to find them. Last night, he had got lost in the thunderstorm. He didn't know that the other frogs were in the muddy pond over the Big Field.

Duggy Dog yawned and got to his feet.
"Follow me," he told the new frog.
And off they went, Duggy Dog and the
new frog hopping along after him.

Floss was playing on the Big Field. So
were Minty and little Jasper.

They laughed when they saw Duggy
Dog with the hoppity frog.

"Where are you going, Duggy Dog?"
said Floss.

"To the muddy pond," said Duggy
Dog.

So they all ran with him. Over the Big
Field they raced, Duggy Dog and his
friends. The new frog tried to keep up
with them, but they were too fast for him.

"Wait for me, Duggy Dog!" he called.

Duggy Dog looked back.

"It isn't far," he told the new frog.
"We're nearly there."

Duggy Dog didn't know how near he
was to the pond.

Suddenly, he felt himself flying through the air. The ground had gone from under his feet. His legs still kept on running, but there was nothing to run on.

"Where has the ground gone?" said Duggy Dog.

Then, with a huge *splashhh!* he landed in the muddy pond.

The new frog followed him into the
pond. Dozens and dozens of other new,
shiny, green frogs croaked back at the
new frog and Duggy Dog.

The new frog told them how kind
Duggy Dog had been.

"Kind?" growled Duggy Dog. He
splashed to the bank. "I suppose I am,
sometimes."

Floss and Minty and little Jasper
looked at him in amazement. Why had
Duggy Dog kept on going, into the pond?

"I just didn't see the pond," said Duggy
Dog. "I think I was still half-asleep. But I
feel wide-awake now!"

They all laughed and laughed, until
Duggy Dog shook himself and drenched
them.

"Goodbye Duggy Dog," called the new
frog, as he swam off with his friends.

"Goodbye," growled Duggy Dog, but
it was a friendly sort of growl.

He didn't feel sleepy any longer. The new frog was right. You could sleep any old time.

"Come on," he said to Floss and Minty and Jasper. "Let's play chase."

And that's what they did, all day long.

Also available in First Young Puffin

BELLA AT THE BALLET
Brian Ball

Bella has been looking forward to her first ballet lesson
for ages – but she's cross when Mum says Baby
Tommy is coming with them. Bella is sure Tommy will
spoil everything, but in the end it's hard to know who
enjoys the class more – Bella or Tommy!

WHAT STELLA SAW
Wendy Smith

Stella's mum is a fortune-teller who always gets things
wrong. But when football-mad Stella starts reading tea
leaves, she seems to be right every time! Or is she . . .

THE DAY THE SMELLS WENT WRONG
Catherine Sefton

It is just an ordinary day, but Jackie and Phil can't
understand why nothing smells as it should. Toast
smells like tar, fruit smells like fish, and their school
dinners smell of perfume!
Together, Jackie and Phil discover the cause of
the problem . . .